Foster Families

THE CHANGING FACE OF MODERN FAMILIES

Foster Families

Julianna Fields

Mason Crest Publishers, Inc.

MASON CREST PUBLISHERS INC.
370 Reed Road
Broomall, Pennsylvania 19008
(866)MCP-BOOK (toll free)
www.masoncrest.com

First Printing

9 8 7 6 5 4 3 2 1

ISBN 978-1-4222-1497-8
ISBN 978-1-4222-1490-9 (series)
Library of Congress Cataloging-in-Publication Data
Fields, Julianna.

Produced by Harding House Publishing Service, Inc. www.hardinghousepages.com
Interior Design by MK Bassett-Harvey.
Cover design by Asya Blue www.asyablue.com.
Printed in The United States of America.

Although the families whose stories are told in this book are made up of real people, in some cases their names have been changed to protect their privacy.

Photo Credits

Dreamstime: Coman, Lucian: p. 16, Cotton, Alistair: p. 15, Kacso, Sandor: p. 39, Losevsky, Pavel: p. 52, Malov, Andrei: p. 44; Monkey Business Images: p. 10, Nelson, Richard: p. 53, Thoermer, Val: p. 26, Willeecole: p. 56

Contents

Introduction

The Gallup Poll has become synonymous with accurate statistics on what people really think, how they live, and what they do. Founded in 1935 by statistician Dr. George Gallup, the Gallup Organization continues to provide the world with unbiased research on who we really are.

From recent Gallup Polls, we can learn a great deal about the modern family. For example, a June 2007 Gallup Poll reported that Americans, on average, believe the ideal number of children for a family to have these days is 2.5. This includes 56 percent of Americans who think it is best to have a small family of one, two, or no children, and 34 percent who think it is ideal to have a larger family of three or more children; nine percent have no opinion. Another recent Gallup Poll found that when Americans were asked, "Do you think homosexual couples should or should not have the legal right to adopt a child," 49 percent of Americans said they should, and 48 percent said they shouldn't; 43 percent supported the legalization of gay marriage, while 57 percent did not. Yet another poll found that 34 percent of Americans feel a conflict between the demands of their professional life and their family life; 39 percent still believe that one parent should ideally stay home with the children while the other works.

Keep in mind that Gallup Polls do not tell us what is right or wrong. They don't report on what people should think—only on what they do think. And what is clear from Gallup Polls is that while the shape of families is changing in our modern world, the concept of family is still vital to our sense of who we are and how we interact with others. An indication of this is the 2008 Gallup poll that found that three out of four Americans reported that family values are important, while one in three said they are "extremely" important.

And how do Americans define "family values"? According to the same poll, here's what Americans say is their definition of a family: a strong unit where faith and morals, education and integrity play important roles within the structure of a committed relationship.

The books in the series demonstrate that strong family units come in all shapes and sizes. Those differences, however, do not change the faith, integrity, and commitment of the families who tell their stories within these books.

1 Growing Up in Foster Care

Aisha's parents are homeless, and since they cannot provide a safe home for their children right now, Aisha and her brothers and sisters were placed in a foster family. Terry's mother is in prison, serving a life sentence, and after she gave birth to him, Terry went to live with a foster family. Lisa was placed with foster parents after her biological father repeatedly abused her. Dwayne's mom has a drug problem, so he and his sisters are living with a foster family while his mother goes through a *rehabilitation program*.

For one reason or another, foster children have been removed from their birth parents by *state* authority. Their families are not safe places for them, and so social services finds them another family. Foster parents receive financial support from the government in return for providing care for these children.

Foster families are not intended to be permanent; they are meant to be a short-term alternative on the way to one of three outcomes:

- being reunited with the biological parent or parents, once the parents have worked out whatever problems interfered with their ability to provide a safe home for their children.
- *termination* of *parental rights* (a formal legal procedure) to be followed, hopefully, by adoption.
- long-term care with foster parents or relatives.

One of these three outcomes is always the goal for children in foster care, and most states do all they can to help birth parents and children solve their problems so they can once more be a family. Unfortunately, however, all too often none of these possible outcomes can be achieved.

Terms to Understand

social phobia: extreme fears involving various situations in which others may criticize you, such as speaking in public, eating in front of others, etc.
panic syndrome: a disorder characterized by extreme panic attacks, in which a person experiences a variety of symptoms such as fear, dizziness, nausea, rapid heartbeat, sweating, or a feeling of choking.
GED: General Equivalency Diploma; earned by taking a series of tests, the GED is equivalent to a high school diploma.
alumni: former students, employees, or members of a group.
resilient: able to recover from difficulties in life, serious illnesses, or other hardships.
developmental disability: life-long physical or mental impairments affecting a person's ability to learn, move around, or live independently.
cerebral palsy: a disorder caused by an injury to the brain before or during birth, causing difficulty controlling the voluntary muscles.
wards: children, or those who are mentally incompetent, in the guardianship of another, not their parents and often the court system.

Foster Children

Sometimes, a child may move from foster home to foster home throughout her growing-up years. These circumstances can damage a young person's self-esteem and sense of security.

Being removed from their homes and placed in foster care is a difficult and stressful experience for children. Many of these children have already suffered some form of serious abuse or neglect before entering foster care— so it's no wonder that about a third of the children in foster care have serious emotional, behavioral, or devel-

Most children entering the foster care system have already experienced major loss and hardship in their lives.

opmental problems. Physical health problems are also common.

Children in foster care often struggle with the following issues:

- blaming themselves and feeling guilty for their removal from their birth parents
- wanting to return to birth parents even if they were abused by them
- feeling unwanted if awaiting adoption for a long time
- feeling helpless about multiple changes in foster parents over time
- having mixed emotions about attaching to foster parents
- feeling insecure and uncertain about their future
- reluctantly acknowledging positive feelings for foster parents

Foster Parents

Foster parents open their homes and hearts to children in need of temporary care. This can be both rewarding and painful. Important challenges foster parents must face include:

- recognizing the limits of their emotional attachment to the child
- understanding mixed feelings toward the child's birth parents

Children may be placed in foster care for a variety of reasons. Some of the most common include:

- abuse and/or neglect
- abandonment
- a parent's emotional or physical illness
- a parent's alcohol/ substance abuse
- a parent's *incarceration*
- a parent's death
- a child's severe behavioral problems

- recognizing their difficulties in letting the child return to birth parents
- dealing with the complex needs (emotional, physical, etc.) of children in their care
- working with sponsoring social agencies
- finding needed support services in the community
- dealing with the child's emotions and behavior following visits with birth parents

Two out of three children who enter foster care are reunited with their birth parents within two years. A significant number, however, can spend long periods of time in care awaiting adoption or other permanent arrangement.

What Do You Think?

Why do foster parents have mixed feelings about the biological parents of their foster children? Why do foster children feel guilty? Why might both foster children and foster parents be reluctant to become attached to each other?

Unfortunately, the number of available foster parents has decreased over the past ten years, and this means that more children end up in *institutions*. Group homes or residential facilities settings can range in size from six children to more than a hundred. Research has shown that children who live in group homes or other facilities are likely to have poorer health than those placed in family foster homes; they're also more apt to experiment with risky behaviors such as substance abuse and early sex. Not all foster families are perfect, but children who grow up in institutions may have an even harder time developing positive self-images and stable emotional well-being. Sometimes, however, a child's problems may be so severe that they interfere with his ability to live in a family setting. These may include serious emotional, physical, or intellectual disabilities.

DID YOU KNOW?
Over 500,000 children in the U.S. currently reside in some form of foster care.

When Foster Kids Grow Up

Children who grow up in foster care are less likely to make the transition successfully into adulthood. Many drop out of school; they may face *discrimination* and poverty; they often lack important life skills; and they frequently don't have adults who can guide and support them into the responsibilities of adulthood.

Growing up in a foster home is hard. These kids face extraordinary challenges in the areas of mental health,

Where Do Foster Care Children Live?

Children in foster care grow up in a variety of settings, with many different individuals involved in their lives. Of the half a million young people in foster care, about 45% are placed with relatives, while about 39% are in non-kinship foster homes. The remainder of children in out-of-home care (16%) are in group homes or residential institutions.

Youth in Residential and Group Homes

According to recent findings from the U.S. Department of Health and Human Services, adolescents in residential and group foster homes are among the most troubled children: more of them experience problems at school (57%), and suffer skill deficits (22%). They are aggressive (66%), involved in delinquent behavior (34%), and have substance use problems (31%); almost half are victims of abuse or neglect, and about one-fifth experience post-traumatic stress disorder. Almost two-thirds of these youth have been referred to residential placement from the social service or juvenile justice systems.

education, employment, and finances. The following statistics tell a tragic story:

- A majority (just under four-fifths) of adults formerly in foster care have significant mental health disabilities (depression, *social phobia*, *panic syndrome*, anxiety), with one in four (25.2%) experiencing post-traumatic stress disorder (PTSD) within the previous twelve months.

- The employment rate of adults who were once in the foster care was also lower than that of the general population, with no more than 45% of young adults released from foster care in the past four years reporting earnings in any one quarter over a thirteen-quarter period of one study.

DID YOU KNOW?
There are about 12 million people living in the United States today who grew up in foster care.

People who have grown up in foster care are more likely to be employed in lower-paying day-laborer jobs than to have salaried positions.

Childhood is an important time in an individual's life. Children need secure homes to grow up physically and emotionally healthy. Children who lack this stability often experience problems later in life.

- A high number of former foster care youth changed schools seven times or more from elementary through high school, and many earned a *GED* and not a regular diploma.
- One-third of former foster care youth have incomes at or below the poverty level.
- The pregnancy rate for teenage girls in foster care is more than double the rate of their peers outside of the foster care system.
- Many foster care youth exit the system without any stable housing lined up for them. Almost a quarter end up homeless.
- Researchers have found that just under four-fifths of all adult foster care *alumni* have significant mental health disabilities.

Childhood is an important time in our lives—and what happens then shapes us forever. Children are amazingly *resilient*, and many are able to overcome some of the most difficult challenges and go on to be successful adults.

Foster families can play an important role in helping them to meet these challenges—or they can make life even harder for children like this. There are all kinds of foster families in the world, and each child's story is different.

Of the more than 500,000 children in foster care, 30 to 40% are also in special education. One study estimated that between 20 and 60% of young children entering foster care have a *developmental disability* or delay. These types of disabilities include *cerebral palsy*, mental retardation, and learning disabilities, as well as speech, hearing, and vision impairments. This compares with an estimate of about 10% among the general population.

HEADLINES

(From "Maria and Domingo Sanchez," Foster Care, www. fostercaremonth.org/SuccessStories/PeopleMakingADifference/Pages/ MariaDomingoSanchez.aspx)

Maria and Domingo Sanchez are Mexican immigrants who became U.S. citizens in the hopes of building a better life. As their two children grew older, the couple began to think about becoming foster parents as a way of helping other less fortunate youth.

In 2006, Maria received a life-changing call from the staff at Casey Family Programs in San Diego. As a Catholic, she felt the timing of this call was particularly significant as it came on Holy Thursday with the celebration of Easter only days away. The agency staff told Maria that there was an emergency case involving five siblings for which they were seeking temporary shelter. After many calls to other parents, the agency told her that the Sanchez family was "their last hope" for keeping the kids together. Maria remembers: "We already had our foster parent license and we knew we wanted to help children. But we didn't expect that they would come in bundles of five!"

Maria immediately tried to contact her husband. As a police officer, he typically worked in the field on assignment and was very hard to reach. On that day, however, Domingo answered the phone right away. Maria explained the crisis situation and her husband just laughed and laughed thinking she was joking about the number of children. He agreed to care for all of children, but reminded his wife that she would have to shoulder most of the daily responsibility because of his work schedule.

The children's story was heartbreaking. Prior to living with the Sanchez family, they had been placed in multiple foster homes. Their birth mother was a Mexican citizen who was living in the U.S. illegally. She had seven children, all of whom were born in America, most to different fathers. When the children became *wards* of the court due to abuse and neglect, the mother became frustrated by the system, and fled to Mexico with the children. Maria says:

"She soon realized that she couldn't provide food, clothing and shelter for the kids. They were living in Tijuana, and one by one, the older children ran away and came back to America and re-entered foster care. The oldest son and his foster parent at the time went back to Mexico to convince the mother to let the younger kids leave, too."

Maria admits that being a foster mother to five was overwhelming at first. Her house was suddenly occupied by three teenagers, and two younger girls ages 11 and 8. She and her husband have provided a stable, nurturing home life these children had never

known before. After only a year, two of the children are enrolled in gifted programs at school and one of the older girls is finishing her freshman year at San Diego State University. Maria and Domingo also enrolled the children in a swim club where they have gone from complete beginners to competitive swimmers. Maria adds: "We hope the children will stay with us until they go to college. Even after that, they will always have a home with our family."

What Do You Think?

How do you think Maria and Domingo's foster children will make the transition into adulthood? Why? Would you want to be a foster parent when you're an adult? Why or why not?

HEADLINES

(From "Couple Finds Calling Caring for Foster Children" by Tiffany Green, *Cullman Times*, May 22, 2009.)

Larry and Sherril Hill knew God had a plan for their lives. After their three sons had grown up and moved away from home, they felt the calling to help other children.

"Cullman is such a wonderful place to raise a family, people forget there are so many severely abused children who need a loving home," Sherril said.

In Cullman County alone there are 178 foster children in the custody of the Department of Human Resources.

After seeing the need and feeling the call, she and her husband began the process of becoming therapeutic foster parents.

Therapeutic foster care is more individualized foster care when the child has a diagnosis of post-traumatic stress syndrome, depression, anxiety disorders, defiance disorders or other severe problems.

"You first want to have pity on them, but they need a safe, secure, loving home," she said.

Children in therapeutic foster care are usually placed alone or with siblings with families who have been specially trained to work with children with more severe problems. The homes provide a more structured environment where children can learn social and emotional skills.

The Hills have been doing foster parenting for two and a half years now. . . . "The children are usually on the extreme end of abuse," Sherril said. "If you hear their stories, you would swear there is no one that could do that."

The Hills have grown attached to the 11-year-old girl currently living with them. Sherril said when a child is up for adoption, the foster family does get a say.

"I would like the children I foster to get the best family for them," she said.

Sherril does not want age to hinder someone's decision about fostering a child.

"People have the misconception that foster parenting is for young families," she said.

With special classes and training, almost anyone can become a foster parent.

"I want to encourage people with grown kids to have a willingness to open their hearts and homes," she said. "It you have a spare room, you can do it."

What Do You Think?

Why do you think many people are reluctant to take in foster children, especially ones with more severe problems like those described in this article?

2 A Real Family

Belinda Howe has two mothers—Mom and Ma—but Ma is her *real* mother, the one who has always been there for Belinda. Mom is just the woman who gave birth to her.

When Belinda was nine, her biological mother admitted she could no longer handle the stress of taking care of Belinda and her two little sisters. Mom liked to drink, she liked to date, and she liked to stay out all night. Belinda ended up being the baby sitter for days on end for Neesie, who was only three, and Debbie, who was five. When the neighbors found out, they called *Social Services*. A *child protective worker* started visiting their home regularly, working with their mother to help her better understand her responsibilities. But the girls' mother had her own problems: she was only twenty-five, and she'd never had anyone who had showed her how to be a good mother; her own mother had abandoned her family. Finally, when the

> ## Terms to Understand
>
> ***Social Services:*** an informal name for a government agency that works on behalf of children, investigating reports of abuse or neglect, and handling foster care and adoptions.
> ***child protective worker:*** a social worker who focuses on the needs of children dealing with neglect or abuse.
> ***custody:*** care, keeping, guardianship.
> ***prowess:*** exceptional and superior skill or ability.
> ***philanthropic:*** acting to help people out of love for humanity.

child protective worker found the girls alone with very little food in a dirty apartment for the third time, she made the decision to take the girls into custody. Their mother didn't object. In fact, she admitted later, she was relieved.

During that first six weeks in foster care, the three girls were split up. Every night, Belinda lay awake worrying about her little sisters. Even though she was only nine years old, she felt like she was grown up compared to Neesie and Debbie. She was the one who had made them brush their teeth and get in their pajamas, the one who listened to them say their prayers at night, and who comforted them when they had bad dreams. Belinda's stomach hurt all night because she was so worried—but that didn't keep her from eating. It seemed so good to finally have plenty of food, after years of eating nothing but crackers and cookies and soda. That's what Belinda remembers best about those weeks: the food. By the time their social worker picked her up to drive her to her new foster placement, Belinda's blue jeans were cutting into her waist and her T-shirts fit her like a second skin.

Belinda was excited to learn that Neesie and Debbie would be with her at the new foster home. And when Thelma Finch opened the door and greeted them, Belinda loved her on the spot.

Thelma—or Ma, as the girls learned to call her—was in her fifties and had already raised two adult sons who no longer lived at home. She wore glasses and aprons over her housedresses; in Belinda's mind, Ma looked exactly the way a mother should look: sweet and gentle and a little frumpy. Her husband—Daddy Dan, the girls called him—was a quiet man who went to work and seldom spoke, but Ma chattered and sang while she cooked and cleaned. She fussed over the girls, bought them new clothes, and baked them cookies. By the end of their first week with Ma, the girls felt as though they had landed in a dream world, the place where they

Length of Time Children Stay in Foster Care Facilities

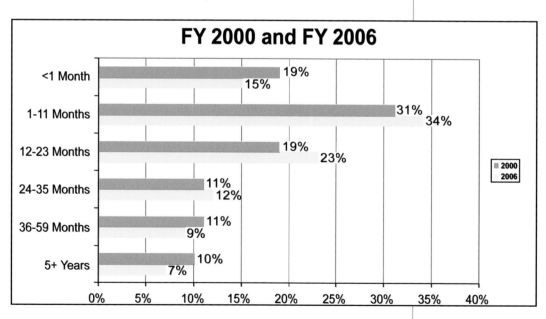

Helping with everyday family chores can help foster children gain a sense of stability and adjust to their new home.

had always longed to live. Daddy Dan brought them home a puppy, Ma helped them with their homework, and their new big brothers teased them and brought them CDs when they visited on the weekends.

But even though Belinda was happier than she would ever have believed possible, she couldn't believe that their new home would last. At night, she still lay awake and worried about what would happen next. Sooner or later, she feared, Ma would get tired of them and give them back. Belinda's stomach still ached all the time—and she still ate constantly, as though she were making up for the years of hunger. Neesie and Debbie were as skinny as little sticks, but Belinda was turning into a round little girl.

And then one day after school, Ma asked Belinda to come upstairs with her. Belinda's stomach hurt so bad that she felt like a knife was turning around and around in her belly. Ma pulled open the drawer where Belinda kept her underwear and socks. She moved aside the clothes. "What's this, Belinda?"

Belinda's eyes filled with tears. She looked down at the pieces of cake, the hamburgers, the pancakes, the pieces of cheese, all wrapped in paper towels, that she'd hidden at the back of the drawer. "Sometimes," she whispered, "I get hungry at night."

Ma would send her away now, she was sure of it. Maybe she would at least keep the little girls, though. After all, they hadn't done anything wrong, only Belinda.

Ma sat down on Belinda's bed. She took Belinda's hand and pulled her down next to her. "When do you get this food, Belinda?"

Belinda stared down at the floor. "At night. When everyone's asleep."

"Belinda, you know you can eat as much as you want at meal times, don't you? And you're always welcome to get a snack from the kitchen. But this food is stale. The meat will go bad if you keep it here. Your room will start to smell."

"I'm sorry," Belinda wailed, tears rolling down her face. "Please don't send me away.

Ma took Belinda in her arms. "I'm not going to send you away, child! But I don't understand why you've been

Compulsive Overeating

People who eat compulsively have an eating disorder, a psychological condition. There are different types of eating disorders (some people eat too much, some too little), but generally, eating disorders involve self-critical and negative thoughts about the individual's body, as well as eating habits that disrupt normal body function and daily activities. While more common among girls, eating disorders can affect boys, too. They're so common in the United States, that one or two out of every hundred kids struggles with some form of eating disorder. Bulimia and anorexia are two other kinds of eating disorders.

People like Belinda who eat compulsively use food and eating as a way to hide from their emotions, to fill an emptiness they feel inside, and to cope with daily stresses and problems in their lives. Food has become their addiction.

People suffering with this eating disorder tend to be overweight, and they are usually aware that their eating habits are abnormal. Words like, "just go on a diet" can be emotionally devastating to a person with this disorder because it's not that simple for her. People who are compulsive overeaters often feel guilty for not being "good enough"; they're ashamed that they're overweight, and they generally have a very low self-esteem—and then they use food and eating to cope with these feelings all over again, creating a vicious cycle.

hiding food away like a little squirrel. Promise me you won't do it anymore."

Belinda promised, but over the years, she often broke her promise. Sometimes, she felt as though there was an empty hole inside her and the only way she knew how to fill it was with food. She worried that one day when she had that feeling, there would be no food around to fill her emptiness, and so she continued to keep a secret stash of candy bars and cookies beneath her bed and at the back of her closet.

When Belinda was thirteen, Ma took in another foster child, this time a baby named Jamie. Jamie had been born with something wrong with his esophagus, and he had already needed to have many operations in his short life. Ma and the girls adored Jamie, and Belinda especially loved taking care of him. He had huge brown eyes with eyelashes an inch long, and his smile always eased the pain in her stomach. Taking care of Jamie helped fill that empty hole inside Belinda, and she didn't need to eat as much anymore.

Jamie had delayed development, the social worker told them, but with lots of love and encouragement, he was learning to walk and talk. And then one day when the girls got off the school bus, they found Ma holding Jamie with tears running down her face. "We have to give him back to his mother," she explained.

Belinda was furious. She was sure that Jamie's biological mother wouldn't take care of him. He had

to eat special foods, and he needed lots of attention. Belinda tried to persuade Ma to run away with Jamie. "We could all move to Canada," she insisted. "Or Mexico."

But Ma just smiled sadly and shook her head, and the day came when they had to say good-bye to Jamie. Belinda cried so hard she made herself sick. After that she started eating all the time again, and by the time she was fifteen, she weighed nearly two hundred pounds. Ma made sure she always had pretty clothes to wear, but the other kids at school still teased her about being so fat. Belinda hated her body—but she couldn't seem to stop herself from eating.

The family prayed for Jamie every day. Even if he no longer lived with them, he was still a part of their family, Ma said, and Belinda agreed.

One day, when Jamie was nearly three, Ma got a phone call. Jamie was in the hospital and was very sick. He had been eating popcorn, and it had torn his fragile esophagus. He would need another surgery before he could be released from the hospital—but the social worker wondered if Ma would be willing to take him back once he was well enough.

The entire family was delighted. They went to visit Jamie in the hospital, and they got his room ready for him to come home. And the best thing was that they would get to keep him this time. "His mother has agreed to release him for adoption," Ma explained to the girls.

Belinda knew that Ma would have liked to adopt her and her sisters as well, but Mom refused to give up all her rights to her children. The girls visited their biological mother once a month. They usually met with her with the social worker; sometimes they would go to a movie or walk around the mall with her. Belinda wor-

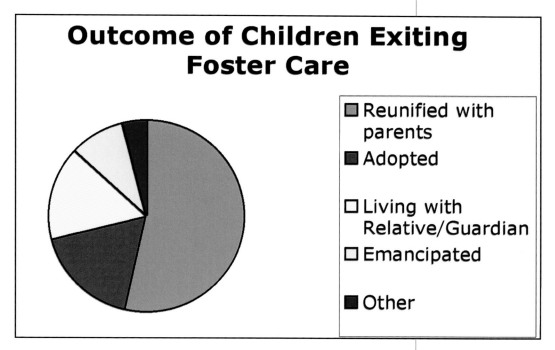

Possible outcomes for children leaving foster care.

ried that one day, Mom would decide she wanted to take the girls back.

But as the years went by, Belinda realized her mom was never going to do that. Belinda, her sisters, and Jamie truly belonged to a family now. No matter what happened, she knew that Ma would always be there for them.

That didn't mean that all Belinda's problems went away. Her emotional scars were deep and painful, and she continues to struggle with her relationship with food. But Belinda is happy watching Jamie and her little sisters grow older, and she does her best to protect them from the problems that have bothered her.

"Families aren't perfect," Ma always reminds her. "But they do their best for each other."

What Do You Think?

How is Belinda's problem with her weight connected to her past? Do you think she will ever be able to overcome her eating problems? What do you think Belinda might have been like if she had not come to live with Ma?

HEADLINES

(From "Keith Bulluck," Foster Care, www.fostercaremonth.org/
SuccessStories/FosterCareAlumni/Pages/KeithBulluck.aspx)

NFL star Keith Bulluck is one guy who isn't afraid to take on a challenge. Whether he's chasing down a scrambling quarterback on the gridiron or helping those less fortunate in the community, this seven-year defensive standout for the Tennessee Titans brings a winning attitude and positive energy to everything he does.

A fan favorite, Keith is a proven leader both on and off the field. His athletic *prowess* has earned him All-Pro honors most notably his outstanding tackling ability. In fact, he ranks third on the Titan's all-time tackle list with more than 1,027 stops. Equally impressive is Keith's dedication to helping others. His teammates, members of the media and local non-profit executives recently honored Keith by naming him the Titan's "Walter Payton Man of the Year" for his outstanding community service in both 2006 and 2007.

Keith has overcome many obstacles in his life to become a hero in the eyes of children, as well as adults. At the age of 12, Keith was placed in foster care when his own mother was going through a difficult time and could no longer care for him. The stay,

which was supposed to last three weeks, turned into six years. Keith recalls:

> "You have to play the cards you're dealt. I tried to keep my head level and just persevere. I went to live with Linda Welch, a single woman originally from England. My foster mother and I came from such different cultures. But she gave me the stability and support I needed to excel in school."

Keith attended Syracuse University on a scholarship and graduated with a bachelor's degree in psychology. In 2000, he fulfilled his dream of playing professional football when the Titans selected the talented linebacker as their first-round draft choice.

During the off-season, Keith focuses his time on *philanthropic* efforts that benefit children in foster care. In 2003, he founded the Believe and Achieve Foundation to help foster youth in Tennessee and New York. He hosts charity fundraisers, toy drives and holiday parties for youth in foster care and their families. He regularly visits schools to sign autographs, donate supplies and speak about the importance of education in getting ahead in life. His foundation also has developed a computer program with New Horizon Technology to help young adults who are transitioning out of foster care with technical job training skills. Keith says:

"Young people in foster care often figure they will be stuck in minimum-wage jobs after they leave the system. I'm proof it doesn't have to be that way. Sure, I had natural ability, size and a lot of breaks, but you also need focus in life, someone to bring you along, someone to help you develop job skills."

What Do You Think?

Keith indicates that the stability and support he received from his foster mother was more important than the fact that she was from a very different cultural background than he was. Why do you think that was true? Why do you think Keith wants to help foster children like himself?

HEADLINES

(From "Want to Make a Difference? Foster a Teen" by Mary Lee, *Clinton News*, May 21, 2009.)

Who would help me? That's what I was wondering almost 15 years ago. I was 12 years old and so scared when I entered the foster care system due to abuse and neglect.

I became one of the thousands of "older children" in the foster care system. . . . While there is a need for foster parents for all ages, the most desperate need is always for people willing to help older children and teens.

By becoming a foster parent to an older child or teen, you may be the biggest influence on the kind of person they will become. You can be the one who teaches them how to live: how to cook spaghetti, balance a checkbook or change a tire.

They may discover their spirituality by watching how you live your life and following your example. You can teach them to build healthy relationships, a skill that will be essential as they move on to adult life. Most of all, you'll show them what it really means to be a part of a family: both the rewards and the responsibilities.

. . . For a long time, I thought I would be on my own after foster care. Every six months, I would go before a juvenile court judge to have my case reviewed. It was mostly a formality, but when I was 16, the judge asked: "Mary, what do you want for your life?"

My response, "I want what everyone else wants. I want a forever family. I want to be adopted."

At that time, there was little emphasis on finding families for older foster children. In fact, people asked me why I would put myself out there and risk possible rejection. I told them that I wanted a forever family. I wanted a place to go home to during Christmas breaks, a dad to walk me down the aisle, and grandparents for my children. Life is so much more than just childhood. Adults rely on their families too.

My adoption was finalized a week before my 18th birthday.

Adoption is becoming a reality for more and more older foster children now. Still, thousands age out of foster care each year without family support.

In the end, many people stepped up to help me grow from a frightened little girl in foster care to a successful adult. There were my foster parents, case workers, counselors, mentors and finally, my wonderful parents. It was a difficult journey, but I ended up where I desperately wanted to be, in a forever family that will be here for me all of my life.

What Do You Think?

Why is a "forever family" important, no matter how old you are?

3 Journey into the Past

Jeff peered through his blue-framed glasses out the window as his car crawled down the center of the street. "I'll be darned. Does that say 'Windsor'?" He stepped on the brake and crept to the curb, got out and bounded up the cracked sidewalk to a peeling front door, his gray ponytail snaking down his back. Winter's cold rain had turned the grass to muddy brown, and scraps of wet paper clung to the mud. Dirty drapes hung cockeyed in the smudged picture window.

Jeff remembered the house had looked just as shabby years ago.

A second after he knocked, an unshaven man in a battered wheelchair opened the door. "Yeah?"

"I'm Jeff. As in Jeff Windsor. Is Maureen or Sherm here?"

"You're kiddin' me. Jeff! How are you? Come on in! The old man's in the kitchen."

Terms to Understand

traumas: physical or psychological shocks or injuries.
apathetic: uninterested, unconcerned, indifferent.
versatile: capable of doing many things well.
iconic: having great cultural significance.
transition: the movement from one state or position to another.

As Jeff followed the man in the wheelchair down a dim hallway, he introduced himself as Jimmy, one of Sherm and Maureen's twin sons.

An unhappy-looking black mongrel with a pit bull jaw sniffed Jeff's legs.

"Don't let him bite you. He can get an attitude," Jimmy said.

A ripped sheet was tacked up in front of the stairs, and laundry, boxes, papers littered the edges of the

In good foster situations, foster children can maintain a close relationship with their foster parents throughout their lives.

Foster Care and the Law

In the United States, foster home licensing requirements vary from state to state, but they are generally overseen by each state's Department of Social Services.

A law passed by Congress in 1961 allowed Welfare payments to pay for foster care which was previously made only to children in their own homes. This provided funding for foster parents and institutions—and foster care placements grew rapidly. Some experts have noted that this gives people and agencies an *incentive* to keep children in foster care. A National Coalition for Child Protection Reform issue paper states that "children often are removed from their families prematurely or unnecessarily because federal aid formulas give states a strong financial incentive to do so rather than provide services to keep families together."

In 1997, President Bill Clinton signed a new foster care law, the Adoption and Safe Families Act (ASFA), which reduced the time children are allowed to remain in foster care before being available for adoption. The new law requires state

floor. Jeff followed Jimmy toward the light spilling from the kitchen.

At the table sat a man in his mid-eighties, eyes milky with cataracts. Jimmy wheeled himself across the pit-

child welfare agencies to identify cases where "aggravated circumstances" make permanent separation of child from the birth family the best option for the safety and well-being of the child. One of the main components of ASFA is the imposition of stricter time limits on reunification efforts. Supporters of ASFA claimed that before the law was passed, the lack of such legislation was the reason it was common for children to languish in care for years with no permanent living situation. These children were often moved from placement to placement with no real plan for a permanent home. Meanwhile, opponents of ASFA argue that the real reason children languished in foster care was that too many were taken needlessly from their parents in the first place. Since ASFA did not address this, opponents said, it would not accomplish its goals, and would only slow a decline in the foster care population. Ten years after ASFA became law, the number of children in foster care on any given day is only about 7,000 fewer than when ASFA was passed. All too often, children are still moved from placement to placement until they "age out" of the system.

ted linoleum into his position at the far side of the table.

"Know who this is?" Jimmy yelled in the old man's direction.

"No." No expression, no question on the old man's face. "No."

"It's Jeff!"

"Jeff?" The old face shifted, a look of faint interest entering his eyes. "You're kiddin' me. . ." Sherm's gravelly voice trailed off in wonder. "Jeff!"

"Yep, it's me. How you been doing? Where's Maureen?" The big woman had worn the pants in the family. Maureen had been the man of the house.

"She died two years ago," Jimmy said, answering for Sherm.

Jeff murmured his condolences, but the words did not come from his heart.

"How are you doing, Sherm?" he yelled across the table.

"Eh, not bad. Alive, that's it." The old man's eyes looked glazed. "So you're doing okay?" Whatever Sherm's mental condition, he clearly remembered Jeff.

"Yeah. Okay." Jeff quickly changed the subject to football. The men discussed the relative worth of teams and players.

After twenty minutes, silences lengthened; it was time to go. Jeff wrote down their phone number, then pulled out a business card that read, "Jeffrey A. Hotchkiss, Juris Doctor" with his phone number and address.

Jimmy glanced at the card, looked puzzled, then slid it across the table to his father.

"It must have been, what, the early seventies last time I was here," Jeff said, taking himself on a five-step tour of the kitchen. He looked down into the basement. There was a familiar corner, concrete walls meeting concrete floor. He, always the "bad boy," had stood in that corner often. He remembered Maureen throwing peanut butter and jelly sandwiches down the stairs at him for his lunch. He had been all of five, six, seven years old then.

More Foster Care Law

The Foster Care Independence Act of 1999 helps foster youth who are "aging out" of care to achieve self-sufficiency. The U.S. government has also funded the Education and Training Voucher Program in recent years in order to help youth who age out of care to obtain college or vocational training at a free or reduced cost. The Fostering Connection to Success and Increasing Adoptions Act of 2008 is the most recent piece of major federal legislation intended to improve the foster care system. This bill extended various benefits and funding for foster children between the age of 18 and 21. The legislation also strengthens requirements for states in their treatment of siblings (e.g., it requires states to make a reasonable effort to place siblings together) and introduces mechanisms to financially encourage adoption.

Before Sherm and Maureen had taken him in, he had lived with his biological mother and his stepfather. But when Jeff was three, his stepfather beat him so badly he needed hospitalization. Jeff's major crime was simply that he looked like his biological father, whom his mother and stepfather despised. After he recovered, Jeff never went home again. Child Protective Services put him into foster care, which ended up being a series of more than a dozen placements a year.

The Windsor family had been the last one. They were desperate for a child of their own, and Jeff's face looked very much like that of Maureen. So this time his looks counted in his favor.

Jeff was a difficult child, forever asking questions and exploring to satisfy his enormous curiosity. A social worker noted in his

When no foster family can be found, a child will often be placed in an institutional residence, which lacks the warmth of a home and family.

file that Jeff was also an emotionally damaged child, one who hit his head hard on the coffee table again and again but never cried out in pain. Unfortunately, the Windsors had little education or intelligence to help him overcome the *traumas* of his past.

Maureen had considered him a challenge that she planned to master. She and her husband decided to adopt Jeff—and then, two years later, Maureen conceived twins. Now that she had children of her own now, she didn't need the problem child who would later prove himself to be a genius.

So Jeff was dumped back into the foster care system. Had Sherm wanted to dump him, too? Jeff didn't know, and he would never ask. The years that followed had not been easy. No one wanted a difficult kid who was becoming increasingly angry at life.

Now, as Jeff rose to leave, he was glad he had finally reached adulthood. "You take care now, Sherm," he told the old man. "You too," he said to the man in the wheelchair.

Ten steps took him out the door. He was eager to get back home to his own family.

In the years since he had left the Windsors, he had completed college, then gone on to become a lawyer, practicing under the name he had been given at birth. He married, and he and his wife Janice had three sons, all of whom were at various universities pursuing their own degrees.

It hadn't been easy for Jeff to become a good father. After all, he'd never had an adequate example in his own life. But like everything else in his life, he worked at it. He was determined to rise above his past.

What kind of person would he have become, he wondered now, if he had stayed in the Windsor household? Would his intelligence have been recognized and encouraged—or would Maureen have continued to punish him for his drive to try new things?

Over the years, he had been an unwanted child in many homes with caregivers who were *apathetic*, and with some who were downright abusive. Only one genuinely cared about him; for decades he sent her gifts on every occasion as a constant reminder of his gratitude to her for her kindness.

Now Jeff looked back at the shabby house as he drove away. Sherm was standing in the door, watching. Jeff would never know what he was thinking. He realized he didn't really care.

What Do You Think?

Why did Jeff turn out as good as he did, despite his past? Why do you think Jeff went back to visit the Windsors?

HEADLINES

(From "Victoria Rowell," Foster Care, www.fostercaremonth.org/ SuccessStories/FosterCareAlumni/Pages/VictoriaRowell.aspx)

Film and television star Victoria Rowell works diligently to raise awareness about the issues surrounding foster care. In her poignant memoir, *The Women Who Raised Me* (HarperCollins), she shares her own incredible journey from foster care to fame taking time to honor the people who helped shape her life along the way. The NAACP recently recognized the bestselling book as the 2008 Outstanding Literary Work by a Debut Author.

Victoria is a *versatile* actress of theatre, television and feature films. Her television credits include *The Cosby Show*, *Diagnosis Murder* and her *iconic* role of Drucilla Winters on the CBS daytime drama *The Young and the Restless*. She successfully introduced a foster care storyline into the drama, for which CBS has received several awards and national recognition. Victoria's credits on the silver screen include *The Distinguished Gentleman*, *Dumb and Dumber*, *Eve's Bayou* and the recent war drama *Home of the Brave*. Currently, Victoria is penning her next book, *Secrets of a Soap Opera Diva* and has been busy on the campaign trail supporting presidential candidate Senator Hillary Clinton.

Victoria entered the Maine foster care system as an infant, and lived in a number of homes with nurturing foster parents who helped identify her talents and shape her future career. At the age of sixteen, after eight years of formal training, Victoria received scholarships to the School of American Ballet and American Ballet Theater in New York City. After a series of tours with Ballet Hispanico, the Julliard School of Music and Twyla Tharp Workshops, Victoria began her modeling and acting career.

Success has given Victoria a voice for foster children. She is the recipient of 12 NAACP Image Awards and an inspirational role model to thousands of young people in foster care. In 1990, she formed the Rowell Foster Children's Positive Plan a non-profit organization that provides both job placement opportunities and enrichment programs for children in foster care. In 1998, she became a national spokesperson for Casey Family Services, speaking before legislators, child welfare workers and business leaders across the country.

Victoria takes special interest in helping young people successfully *transition* from foster care to independence. In 2000, she worked with Sony and CBS Television to establish an internship program for foster youth, giving them opportunities to work behind the scenes of some of Hollywood's most successful television programs. Victoria says:

"Young people develop a stronger self-image, build confidence and gain a sense of achievement as they participate in the fine arts, athletics, summer camp and job programs. Just as it was for me, these types of experiences offer essential frameworks for being successful in life."

What Do You Think?

This article states that Victoria is especially interested in helping foster children make the move from foster care to independence. Why do you think this is a hard transition for some young people to make?

Do you think Victoria is right that experiences with art, sports, summer camps, and jobs help foster kids build a sense of confidence and self-esteem? Why or why not?

HEADLINES

(From "Being a Foster Parent Requires Love, Flexibility" by Jacque Kochak, *Auburn Villager*, May 20, 2009)

Over the years, Jerry and Karen Franklin have been foster parents to more than 100 children. The most the couple ever had under their roof at one time was 16 kids, Karen Franklin recalls. "Two were our birth chil-

dren, and 14 were gifts," she said. "Every day hasn't been wonderful, but it isn't with birth children, either."

. . . The Fergusons have been foster parents for some 30 years and received additional training to be therapeutic foster parents in 1996 when LCYDC started the program.

. . . Kids come into therapeutic foster care with diagnoses ranging from attention deficit-hyperactivity disorder to oppositional defiant disorder or bipolar disorder. Some are suffering post-traumatic stress disorder after the death of their parents.

All have ended up in foster care because of abuse, however.

"We have foster parents we have to train because even after all the training they think this child should act like their own children did," said [one Human Resources employee]. "Our expectation is they love the child unconditionally, even if the child is not like their own child was and they don't understand why they do some of the things they do."

What Do You Think?

What does "unconditional love" mean? Why is it so important for foster kids?

4 Foster Failure

Derek is an inmate in prison. He doesn't mind being a prisoner as much as you might think, though. Prison provides him with food and clothing; he takes classes there; he knows his way around. Strangely, prison makes him feel safe.

Derek hasn't felt safe much in his life. His birth-father hit him with a broken broomstick so many times that Derek still bears the scars: a crooked finger that broke and healed without ever being set; a long scar on his forehead where the broomstick split his skin; a lump on his shin that's never gone away. One day when he went to school with his face a mess from his father's blows, his teacher called the authorities. Derek never went home again after that.

But his life didn't get any better. The foster home where he was placed already had four other foster chil-

Terms to Understand

manslaughter: the illegal killing of another person without the intention to do harm.

entrepreneur: a person who organizes and runs a business, taking the risk of its success on him or herself.

charismatic: having personal appeal and charm, such that one can attract and inspire others.

echelons: levels of command or rank.

advocate: a person who speaks or writes in support of a position or cause.

mentoring: acting as a counselor or teacher for those younger or less experienced than oneself.

dren, three of them younger and one older. The older one abused Derek sexually. When his foster mother found out, she sent both boys away.

Next, Derek ended up in with a young couple who were not able to have their own children. The woman was kind to Derek, but her husband was often impatient and angry with him. He made fun of Derek's poor

According to research conducted across the United States, about 25 percent of all children in the foster care system are abused. That's one child out of every four.

grades, and ridiculed Derek because he wasn't good at sports. After a year, the couple decided that Derek wasn't working out, and a social worker came to pick him up.

For several months, Derek stayed at a children's home. No one hit him there, no one made fun of him, and no one abused him—but Derek was lonely. He was glad when he was once more sent to another foster home. He wanted to be a part of a family.

Children in foster care frequently struggle with loneliness and a sense of not belonging.

Post-Traumatic Stress Disorder (PTSD)

PTSD is an anxiety disorder that some people get after seeing or living through a dangerous event. This is likely what Derek experienced when he killed the man who hit him.

When in danger, it's natural to feel afraid. This fear triggers many split-second changes in the body to prepare to defend against the danger or to avoid it. This "fight-or-flight" response is a healthy reaction meant to protect a person from harm. But in PTSD, this reaction is changed or damaged. People who have PTSD may feel stressed or frightened even when they're no longer in danger.

Symptoms include:

- Flashbacks—reliving the trauma over and over, including physical symptoms like a racing heart or sweating. These can be triggered by sounds, smells, or similar events.
- Bad dreams
- Frightening thoughts.
- Feeling emotionally numb
- Being easily startled.
- Losing one's temper easily; feeling constantly tense and ready for danger.

But Derek never found a family. Instead, he moved from foster home to foster home. He was a difficult kid, people said, a behavior problem, a problem student, a kid with a bad attitude. Over the next three years, he was in eight different homes; then he spent more time in a children's home, where he was again sexually abused, this time by a worker. When the worker ended up in prison for molesting a minor, Derek felt sorry; for a while, at least, someone had paid attention to him. He had felt like he was important to someone.

When Derek was sent to a new foster home, he had already made up his mind to hate it. He decided to run away. Anything, he told himself, had to be better than living with jerks.

Derek was sixteen now, old enough, he thought, to get a job. But no one wanted to hire him. He ended up living on the streets. One night, he got angry and broke all the windows of a store that had refused to give him work. The police picked him up, and this time Derek went to a juvenile detention center.

When he was released, Derek once more had nowhere to go. He didn't know anyone who could give him advice; he didn't know what to do. To earn money, he began selling himself for sex.

And then one night, in the middle of a "job," the older man pulled out a stick and hit Derek across the shoulders. Derek flew into a rage and hit back. This

Researchers have found that one in four (25.2%) former foster kids have experienced post-traumatic stress disorder (PTSD) within the previous twelve months. This is much higher even than the rates for war veterans!

time, he wasn't a skinny kid who had to take whatever came at him. This time, he was going to hit back.

When he came to himself, the man lay at his feet dead.

Now, Derek is serving a twenty-year sentence for *manslaughter*. He was never able to figure out how to manage in the outside world, but prison life makes sense to him; it has definite rules he can follow. It doesn't seem so bad to him. He's even completed his high school equivalency finally, and has begun working on a college degree.

Eighty percent of prison inmates have spent time in foster care.

When Derek gets out, he will only be in his forties, still young enough to build a life for himself. He is interested in being an architect; just maybe, he thinks, he'll be able to achieve his goals.

And just maybe, he hopes, someday he'll have a family of his own.

There are more than a million runaway and homeless young people in America today. Every year, close to 11,000 young people run away from foster homes.

What Do You Think?

Why do you think Derek is more comfortable in prison than in the outside world?
What do you think Derek's chances are of being successful once he gets out of prison? Why?

HEADLINES

(From "Tony Shellman," Foster Care, www.fostercaremonth.org/SuccessStories/FosterCareAlumni/Pages/TonyShellman.aspx)

One act of kindness can change an entire lifetime, even if it occurs at the tender age of two. That is what happened to Tony Shellman when a Seattle couple came forward to adopt the little boy from foster care.

As he looks back, this successful *entrepreneur* realizes the greatest fortune of his life came out of very unfortunate circumstances. As an infant, Tony was left

in the care of Catholic Charities because his parents felt they could not adequately provide for a second child. On Christmas Eve 1968, he went home with Lenzie and Betty Shellman, who would later adopt him. Tony recalls:

"I guess it turned out to be my lucky break. I knew I was adopted, but it didn't matter because I was with a loving family in a safe place I could always call home. Not every child in foster care gets that happy ending."

With caring support from his adoptive family, the *charismatic* boy enjoyed a full and active childhood. Later, he pursued a modeling career and ultimately moved to New York to study fashion at the renowned Parson's School of Design. From there, Tony worked long hours making his way up from the showroom to the boardroom. His vision and drive propelled him to the upper *echelons* of urban fashion as the co-founder of the popular Mecca and ENYCE clothing lines.

Today, this masterful marketing executive is regarded as an influential hip-hop trendsetter and fashion innovator. Tony has a flair for developing lifestyle brands that engender a loyal following. In 2004, Black Enterprise magazine chronicled Tony's motivational story as one of their profiles in courage. In 2005, Liz Claiborne, Inc. purchased ENYCE for $114 million. In 2007, Tony launched Parish Clothing, a contemporary menswear line that reflects trends and the happenings of the retro 80's hip hop era with flashy bold colors and unique patterns.

As a spokesperson for National Foster Care Month and Casey Family Programs, Tony is a tireless *advocate* for youth in foster care. He is especially focused on providing career *mentoring*, job skills training and employment opportunities for older youth who are preparing to leave the system.

Amid all the glamour and professional accolades, Tony still considers his family to be his greatest treasure. He says:

"I'm not sure where I would be today without their encouragement. I beat the odds, but there are thousands of young people in foster care right now who don't have that kind of support."

What Do You Think?

Can you explain why Tony turned out so differently from Derek? Why do you think Tony "beat the odds" and Derek didn't?

Find Out More
BOOKS

Askeland, Lori. *Children and Youth in Adoption, Orphanages, and Foster Care: A Historical Handbook and Guide.* Santa Barbara, Cal.: Greenwood Press, 2005.

Craig, Stacie. *Foster Parenting: A Simple Guide to Understanding What It's All About.* Slaton, Tex.: Starik Publishing, 2007.

Gerstenzang, Sarah. *Another Mother: Co-Parenting with the Foster Care System.* Nashville, Tenn.: Vanderbilt University Press, 2007.

Harrison, Kathy. *Another Place at the Table.* New York: Tarcher, 2004.

Krebs, Betsy and Paul Pitcoff. *Beyond the Foster Care System: The Future for Teens.* Piscataway, N.J.: Rutgers University Press, 2006.

Libal, Joyce. *A House Between Homes: Youth in the Foster Care System.* Broomall, Pa.: Mason Crest, 2007.

Osgood, D. Wayne, E. Michael Foster, Constance Flanagan, and Gretchen R. Ruth, eds. *On Your Own Without a Net: The Transition to Adulthood for Vulnerable Populations.* Chicago: University of Chicago Press, 2005.

Rowell, Victoria. *The Women Who Raised Me.* New York: HarperCollins, 2008.

Shirk, Martha. *On Their Own: What Happens to Kids When They Age Out of the Foster Care System*. New York: Basic Books, 2006.

Silverstein, Deborah N. and Susan Livingston Smith, eds. *Siblings in Adoption and Foster Care: Traumatic Separations and Honored Connections*. Santa Barbara, Cal.: Praeger, 2008.

ON THE INTERNET

Foster Angels
www.angelsforfosterkids.org

Foster Care and Adoptive
Community
www.fosterparents.com

Foster Kids Are Our Kids
www.fosterkidsareourkids.org

Kids Are Waiting
www.kidsarewaiting.org

National Foster Care Month
www.fostercaremonth.org

The National Network for
Young People in Foster Care
www.fosterclub.com

Bibliography

American Academy of Child & Adolescent Psychology. "Foster Care." *Facts for Families*. No. 64, May 2005.

Green, Tiffany. "Couple Finds Calling Caring for Foster Children."*Cullman Times*, May 22, 2009.

"Keith Bulluck." Foster Care. www.fostercaremonth.org/SuccessStories/FosterCareAlumni/Pages/KeithBulluck.aspx.

Kochak, Jacque. "Being a Foster Parent Requires Love, Flexibility." *Auburn Villager*, May 20, 2009.

Lee, Mary. "Want to Make a Difference? Foster a Teen." *Clinton News*, May 21, 2009.

"Maria and Domingo Sanchez." Foster Care. www.fostercaremonth.org/SuccessStories/PeopleMakingADifference/Pages/MariaDomingoSanchez.aspx.

National Collaborative on Workforce and Disability for Youth. "Negotiating the Curves Toward Employment: A Guide About Youth Involved in the Foster Care System." National Collaborative on Workforce and Disability for Youth: 2008.

National Resource Center for Family-Centered Practice and Permanency Planning. "Homeless after Foster Care." www.hunter.cuny.edu/socwork/nrcfcpp/info_services/homeless.html

Roman, Nan and Phyllis Wolfe. "Web of Failure: The Relationship Between Foster Care and Homelessness." National Alliance to End Homelessness. April 1, 1995.

"Tony Shellman." Foster Care. www.fostercaremonth.org/SuccessStories/FosterCareAlumni/Pages/TonyShellman.aspx.

"Victoria Rowell." Foster Care. www.fostercaremonth.org/SuccessStories/FosterCareAlumni/Pages/VictoriaRowell.aspx.

Index

About the Author and the Consultant

AUTHOR

Julianna Fields is the pseudonym of a Gannett human interest columnist whose byline has also appeared in *Writer's Digest*, *American History*, *American Woodworker* and hundreds of other publications, as well as educational workbooks and a guidebook about Steamtown, a National Park Service site in Scranton, Pennsylvania. She's also a writing coach and editor.

CONSULTANT

Gallup has studied human nature and behavior for more than seventy years. Gallup's reputation for delivering relevant, timely, and visionary research on what people around the world think and feel is the cornerstone of the organization. Gallup employs many of the world's leading scientists in management, economics, psychology, and sociology, and its consultants assist leaders in identifying and monitoring behavioral economic indicators worldwide. Gallup consultants help organizations boost organic growth by increasing customer engagement and maximizing employee productivity through measurement tools, coursework, and strategic advisory services. Gallup's 2,000 professionals deliver services at client organizations, through the Web, at Gallup University's campuses, and in forty offices around the world.